THE CAFE

by Sarah Pond

The Cafe

Copyright 2019 Sarah Pond

PROLOGUE

As Amy woke up, rubbing her bleary eyes, she turned her head to look at Laurel. She watched the gentle rise and fall of Laurel's chest as she slept, her dark brown, shoulder length hair half covering her face. She gently stroked Laurel's hair back over her ear, so she could look at her. Amy ran her hand through her own cropped honey blond hair, tussled and wayward as usual. Quite how she had ended up in bed with Laurel, she wasn't sure. Obviously, she knew how it had happened from a physical point of view, but that wasn't quite what Amy had been trying to work out in her head. Maybe it had been destined, but Amy didn't really believe in that sort of thing. Her mind wandered to the first time she laid eyes on Laurel at the cafe...

ONE

Amy was walking along the seafront on a brisk, bright January morning. The sea was calm, and the tide quite far out, so that the wet sand in the distance shone where the sun's rays touched the surface. The beach was mostly pebbles, and although it wasn't the prettiest stretch of coast, it was her bit of coast, and she loved it.

Ahead of her, Amy could see the outside seating area of the coastal cafe was deserted, but for two people. They were well wrapped up against the cold, a dog curled up at their feet. They looked like a cosy trio, snuggled up together. As Amy walked past the cafe, she looked to her right, and caught the eye of a woman through the window, who appeared to smile at her. She had been to the cafe before, and walked past it many times, but she didn't remember seeing the woman, and was sure she didn't know her. She must have been smiling at the person she was with, and just happened to look out of the window at the same time. Still, as she went on her way, Amy kept thinking about the woman, although she couldn't say why.

When Laurel had happened to glance out of the window at that precise moment, she couldn't help but hold her breath for a moment, and the smile that followed was so natural. She didn't think that the woman walking by had even noticed her. She idly wondered how many times in life this sort of thing happened. That one person could look at another, and be so captivated by someone, whilst the other continued with their life obliviously.

It was a cold morning, and the woman wore a thick aviator jacket with an orange scarf, and dark jeans which hugged her figure. Her short, thick, blond hair was blown around in various directions by the wind. She thought she was probably a similar age, maybe a bit younger than herself, certainly not over forty. Laurel knew that she had never seen her before, she definitely would have remembered her.

The next day, Amy walked past the cafe again. It was on her usual route into town, when she chose to walk along the seafront, which she usually did. It was often windy along this part of the south coast, but she loved to walk along by the sea. The pier in the distance showed her how far it was to the town.

Over the next few days, Amy walked past the cafe a few times, but didn't see the woman again. Then again, why would she. She must have walked past countless people over the last year, most people liked a seat by the window, looking out to sea. It was quite likely that the woman was a day tripper, and chances were that Amy wouldn't see her again. She was just a random person who happened to look out of the window at a random time.

Amy had only been in Worthing for about a year. At the age of forty, she was trying out a fresh start. She was still finding her way around, but the walk into town from her flat was a favourite, and familiar to her. It was quite a long walk, but what else did she have to do with her time. The fresh sea air was invigorating, and a good way to start the day. She would usually turn right off of the seafront, cutting through the shops towards Liverpool Gardens. Although the job was, in Amy's opinion, boring, she loved where it was based. The small grassed area was nestled like a brief oasis between the hustle and bustle of the main shopping centre and the grand beautiful elegance of the Regency styled buildings standing proud and tall.

Amy was in the coastal cafe having a coffee before work one day. Her hours were part time and flexible, another reason for putting up with the mundane aspect of the work. She particularly liked the cafe because of its rustic feel, with its bare wooden tables and sea view. You could only be at the beach in a place like this.

She had been there for nearly half an hour, absorbed in her book. Now she laid it face down on the table, still open, and was idly looking out of the window. As she turned back to her coffee, she happened to look up. The woman she had seen that time was walking towards her, and Amy felt her heart speed up. As the woman walked by, she smiled and said, 'Hello again,' and continued walking towards the door. Just before she left, she turned again, and smiled at Amy. Then she was gone.

Amy didn't reply, she had been too surprised. Having seen her close up, she definitely didn't know her. So why had she said 'Hello again'? She must have been smiling at Amy that first time, she obviously had seen her. Then she hoped that the woman didn't think she was rude for not responding, she had been taken off-guard, that was all. Still, she felt an unexpected flush of excitement.

Laurel had been thrilled to see the woman in the cafe. She had been back many times over the last few weeks, without one sight of her. She believed in things being meant to be, and something inside told her that she would see the woman again. As she approached the woman's table, she slowed her pace slightly, and greeted her as she walked by. The woman hadn't responded, although Laurel could see that she was a bit surprised. Well, close up, she was as attractive as she had first thought when Laurel had first glimpsed her. Walking by the window as she left, Laurel looked in to where the woman was sitting, and for a brief moment, their eyes met.

Over the following days, life was the same as usual for Amy. Except. Her mind kept wandering back to that brief meeting. Why did the woman keep popping into her mind? Did she really have so little going on in her life, that a couple of moments of eye contact with a stranger were so exciting. But she didn't feel like a stranger. Still, Amy thought she really ought to get a hobby or something. The flat could do with brightening up for a start, it was exactly the same as when she had moved in, beige carpets and walls. It was about time she gave it a personal touch. A lick of paint, some nice pictures on the walls. Yes, that was what was needed.

Laurel had really hoped to see the woman again. Despite her frequent visits, there didn't seem to be any pattern as to when the woman would be there. If she saw a head of tussled blonde hair, her heart rate would increase, and she would feel an excitement bubbling up, only for it to slip away again when the person turned and it wasn't her. Damn, was she becoming a stalker now? Maybe she should have said more last time. Oh come on, get over yourself. It was an attractive woman in a cafe, she's probably straight and married anyway. Well, Laurel was going away for a few weeks. What on earth did she think was going to happen, anyway. She would just forget about her.

It was another three weeks before Amy saw her again. This time she saw her approaching the table, and when the woman smiled, she smiled back. She had a stunning smile.

This time Laurel knew it was her. So, it was another chance. Third time lucky, and all that. She would introduce herself, offer her a drink. She would soon know if the woman wanted to be on her own or not. She could always say no, or make an excuse that she had to be somewhere. Although Laurel was sure that wasn't going to happen.

'Do you mind if I join you?'

'Of course not,' Amy gestured to the seat opposite.

Afterwards, Amy had thought it was unusual, that Laurel had just walked up to her and asked to sit down. At the time, it had just seemed so inevitable.

'I'm Laurel,' and she offered her hand to shake.

'Amy. Well, Amelia, but everyone calls me Amy.'

'That's a beautiful name.' Laurel looked right into Amy's eyes, a searing look, and Amy felt herself flush.

Laurel was still holding her hand, and it felt so soft and warm. Then Laurel let go, and sat down. She looked at Amy, smiling. 'I hope you don't mind me joining you, but I keep seeing you around, so I thought a proper introduction would be nice.' Laurel was just glad to have the opportunity to talk to Amy.

'I don't mind at all.' Amy was intrigued to meet the woman who had begun popping into her mind more and more when she had an idle moment. Which seemed to be quite a lot, come to think of it. Amy came to, to see Laurel looking at her, causing her to blush as she smiled shyly.

'Let me get you another drink. What would you like?'

'That's very kind of you. A coffee, thank you. With cream, please.'

'Okay, I'll be right back.' Amy watched Laurel walk away. She noticed how her hips swayed as she walked.

When Laurel returned with a coffee for each of them, she handed the little ceramic jug of cream to Amy. 'Thank you. I know it's a bit naughty having cream, but why not!'

Laurel smiled at the cheeky look on Amy's face. In that moment, she felt a warm glow of affection for Amy, along with a feeling of something more visceral. 'It's good to treat yourself.'

'Is this your regular cafe?' Amy was interested.

'Most of the time it is.'

Amy cocked her head on one side, 'Do you often buy strangers a drink?'

Laurel laughed out loud, and Amy blushed. 'No, I don't. But somehow you don't seem like a stranger.'

Amy gathered the courage to ask the question that had been playing on her mind. 'When I first saw you here, I was walking past outside. I saw you smile through the window, and I thought you must have been smiling at the person you were with.'

Laurel's reply was softly spoken, her gaze intense, 'No, I most definitely was smiling at you.'

The way that Laurel spoke sent a tingle down Amy's spine. Laurel was still looking at Amy, and she turned away, unsure of where to look. Laurel smiled to herself.

As Amy regained herself, she was able to break the silence, 'It's nice to have company. On my own, I sometimes drive myself to distraction.'

You could drive me wild with desire. The thought came out of nowhere, and although Laurel's heart rate had speeded up, she managed to speak calmly, 'I can't imagine that.' So, she was most likely single, then. 'Do you live nearby?'

Amy nodded, gesturing in a general direction behind her, 'About half an hour walk from here. How about you?'

'Similar, maybe a bit less. In the other direction, though.' Laurel smiled at Amy, and tucked her dark brown hair behind her ear. It just about touched her

11

shoulders, and when she leaned forward it flopped down over one eye.

After some more small talk, Amy noticed Laurel look at her watch. It was a large watch with an old brown strap. Amy thought it looked like a man's watch. Laurel said, 'Unfortunately, I have to go now. I really wish I didn't. Would you like to meet up for coffee again next week?'

'Um, yes, okay.'

Laurel noticed that Amy seemed more hesitant now. 'Shall we say Wednesday at ten thirty?'

Amy gave an awkward smile, 'Okay.'

'Perfect. It was lovely to meet you properly, Amy.'

'You too. Thank you for the drink. It will be my treat next week.'

'I'm looking forward to it. See you then.' She touched Amy's shoulder as she left.

Amy found herself looking forward to the following Wednesday more eagerly as it approached. On Wednesday morning, she woke up feeling excited, and looking forward to the day. It struck her that if coffee with an almost stranger was the highlight of her week, she really needed to get out more. She had begun decorating the flat, and although it was keeping her occupied, it was within four walls with a lot of time to let her mind wander.

Laurel was already at the cafe when Amy arrived. She stood to greet Amy, but thought a kiss on the cheek or a hug might be a bit soon, it wasn't as though they were really friends. Well, not yet, although Laurel hoped that they would be. Amy had a very quiet and gentle way about her which Laurel found very soothing to be around.

'Oh, I'm not late, am I?'

Laurel smiled, 'No, I'm a bit early. I thought I'd grab us a table.' She managed to stop herself saying, I just couldn't wait to see you.

'Great. Now, what would you like to drink?'

Laurel watched as Amy walked towards the counter to order. What was it about Amy that she found so fascinating.

Seated together at the table, Laurel began the conversation. 'Have you always lived here?'

Amy looked down at the table before she answered, 'No. I moved from Kent. I've been here about a year now, I suppose.'

'What made you choose to move here?' Laurel noticed a look of discomfort pass across Amy's face, and was just about to change the subject when Amy answered.

Sighing, Amy looked uncomfortable, 'Things weren't working out where I was. It was time for a change.' She paused, before adding, 'And I love the sea.'

Laurel thought that there was much more to tell, but Amy obviously wasn't ready to talk about it yet. It was hardly surprising, she hardly knew Laurel. 'Sorry, I didn't mean to pry.'

Amy smiled a bit too brightly, 'No, don't be silly. It's a natural question. How about you?'

'I've lived here all my life. I do love to travel, but I always come back here.'

Amy was intrigued, 'Do you live on your own?'

'Yes, I do.' Laurel was encouraged that Amy wanted to know. Then again, she could be reading a bit too much into it. It was a pretty standard getting to know you conversation.

'Do you ever get lonely?' Amy looked directly into Laurel's eyes, and Laurel's heart flipped.

'Sometimes. I love living on my own most of the time, though.'

'I find it hard. I suppose I'm still getting used to it. It's far better than living with the wrong person, though.' She looked down at the table again.

'I imagine it is. Apart from an occasional lodger, I've never really lived with anyone. Well, I did share with a girlfriend for a few months once, but that was a long time ago.'

Amy looked up, 'As in friend who's a girl, or relationship?' She looked flustered, before adding, 'Sorry, that's a bit personal, isn't it?'

Laurel laughed, 'Not at all, I did bring it up! Girlfriend girlfriend. I was in my twenties, and we drifted apart. I'm still waiting for the right person.' Laurel smiled, and looked out of the window.

As Amy looked at Laurel, she realised how comfortable she felt with her, and found herself saying, 'I left my fiancé and moved down here. He was a control freak, and after ten years I'd had enough. It ended amicably enough, and fortunately we didn't have any kids. Although he wasn't right for me, I still find it hard being on my own.'

Laurel touched Amy's arm, 'It's not surprising when you've been in such a long relationship. It will take time to adjust.'

'I thought it would be easier by now. Sometimes it is, and at other times I wonder whether I made the right decision.'

Laurel was sympathetic, 'When you think of your ex, how do you feel?'

Laurel didn't need an answer, she could see from the look on Amy's face. 'It wasn't right. I wasn't happy. Sorry, I don't want to burden you with this.'

'Hey, don't apologise. It's good to talk about things. Not that I can help in the advice department, I've never settled down with anyone for long enough!' Truthfully, the thought of settling down scared the life out of her.

After chatting for another hour or so, Amy said she had a few things to do, and that she was going to head off. 'Thank you, Laurel, for listening to me ramble on. It's been really good to be able to talk about how I've been feeling.'

For the whole conversation, Laurel had been attentive, listening without interrupting, and making Amy feel like she was the most important person in the world. For the first time since she could remember, she felt really listened to.

Laurel smiled warmly, 'Any time, I enjoying talking to you.'

'You make it very easy. It feels like it's all been about me, though.'

'Don't be silly, of course not. It's been fascinating getting to know you.' Amy blushed.

They left the cafe together, and outside, they said goodbye. Laurel pulled Amy into a hug, whispering in her ear, 'Remember, any time. You have my number now, just give me a call if you want to talk.'

Amy felt a tingle down her neck as Laurel spoke softly in her ear. It was very kind of Laurel, but she wasn't going to just ring her up to unload her problems. Still, she did appreciate the offer.

As Amy walked away, Laurel watched her for a while, before turning around and heading home.

As Amy walked along, she replayed their conversation, and thought about how kind and patient

Laurel was. She hardly knows me, she thought, and she's listening to me like an old friend. It was so good to be able to relax and chat. Amy used to socialise quite a bit with her friends many years ago, before she met Rob. Over time, she seemed to have less time to spend with them. Of course, she spent most of her spare time with Rob, and when she wasn't with him, he was always ringing or texting to find out where she was, and in the end it was easier to just stay home or go out with him.

TWO

Over the next few weeks, Amy and Laurel were meeting up regularly. Their coffees became lunches, and sometimes walks along the seafront. Amy found that Laurel was such easy company, and she always looked forward to their meetings. She talked about work, a pretty boring admin job, but it paid the bills. She loved hearing about Laurel's travels abroad, and her work as a journalist. Laurel's life seemed terribly exciting and romantic. Amy thought that she had known Laurel long enough now to ask, 'So, there was never anyone you wanted to settle down with?'

'Not really. I had a lot of fun with some people, but no one I could really see myself with long term.'

'I'm being a bit nosey now, but has it always been women?'

Laurel paused for a moment, 'No, not at first. I never really gave it any thought. I fell for who I fell for, simple as that. And how about you. Has there been anyone since Rob?'

'No. I mean, I've liked people, but I needed some time to myself, then I moved down here. It's hard meeting people sometimes.'

'Well, you met me.'

Amy smiled, 'Yes, I did.'

That smile lit up Laurel's insides. She was as attracted to Amy as she had been that first time she had glimpsed her walking by the cafe. She was sure that Amy had no idea, and she certainly wasn't intending on doing anything about it. Amy was clearly still getting over the end of a long relationship, and what she needed was a friend, not more complication. But oh, how in this moment, she would love to hold Amy's hand, learn forward and gently kiss those lips.

'Laurel?'

'Uh, sorry?' Laurel suddenly came to.

'You looked lost in your own little world, there!'

Laurel blushed, hoping that Amy hadn't noticed. 'Sorry, I got distracted for a moment.'

'What was so enticing? Were you thinking about a past lover!' Amy had an amused look on her face.

'No, nothing really.' Laurel was feeling embarrassed now, and quickly changed the subject.

Amy really enjoyed her coffee mornings and lunches with Laurel. It was a welcome break to the routine of a boring office job, where she still didn't really feel like she fitted in. She was starting to get to know a couple of the people there a bit better, though.

Sometimes she would daydream at her desk, and replay conversations with Laurel which would make her laugh to herself. Laurel really listened to her, and she felt so comfortable in her company. She would talk to her about things that she hadn't told anyone else before. On the morning of a day when Amy was going to see Laurel, she would get a bubble of excitement in her stomach. If she didn't know any better, she would have thought she had a crush on Laurel.

The following month, Laurel had suggested going to the cinema. The Dome was opposite the beach, and not far along the seafront from the cafe. Although Amy loved films, she hadn't been to the cinema since she had moved down to the coast. 'It's beautiful.' Amy looked around in wonder at the grade two listed building. Her eyes swept around, taking in the dark wooden panelling and deep red carpets, the lights and chandeliers in the foyer.

Making their way through the doors, Laurel said, 'I've been coming here since I was a child. It used to be referred to as the old fleapit! I love it here.'

'It's so lovely. I can see why you like it so much.' Amy was taking everything in. The original seats, the balconies, the lights.

Taking their seats towards the back of the auditorium, Laurel and Amy got settled down. Leaning on the arms of the seats, occasionally their bare arms touched. Laurel said, 'Would you like anything? I'm going to get a bottle of water.' As she got up, she touched Amy's bare arm.

'No, thank you.' As Amy watched Laurel leave, she could still feel the electricity buzzing on her skin.

When Laurel returned a few minutes later, Amy felt herself flush, and she was glad that the lighting was dimmed in the cinema.

They had both really enjoyed the film. As they were leaving the cinema, Laurel asked, 'Would you like to come back to mine for a drink?'

Amy hesitated for a moment, 'I'd like to, but I have so much to do this evening. Could we maybe do it another time?'

'Of course.' Laurel hid her disappointment well.

Standing outside the cinema, Amy said, 'Thank you, I really enjoyed that.'

'Me too. Shall we meet again next week? You can come to me then if you fancy it?'

'Lovely, thank you.'

As Amy walked home, she wondered why she had refused going back to Laurel's. She really didn't have that much to do, and was sure that Laurel would know that. Still, she had said it now, there was no point thinking about it.

Amy sent a text to Laurel to rearrange the date for coffee at her place, and it ended up being a couple of weeks later. When the time came around, Laurel was very pleased to see Amy on her doorstep, and gave her a hug in welcome. She sensed something a bit different in Amy, although she wasn't sure exactly what.

Amy had decided to leave it a couple of weeks before she saw Laurel again. She really enjoyed spending time with her, but a part of her worried that she looked forward to it a bit too much. She didn't want to get too reliant on one person. With Rob, it had happened a bit at a time, and in the end her world was being a part of his, and she felt swallowed up along the way. But now, sitting here with Laurel, Amy felt so comfortable, and wondered why she had put off seeing her for this long.

Laurel was so pleased to see Amy again. She had been a bit concerned when she first saw Amy at the door, but now she seemed more relaxed, and it was as if no time had passed since they had seen each other. The conversation flowed easily, and the hours slipped by. Whilst they were talking, Amy had told Laurel that she had finished painting her flat. Is that a bit of paint on your hand?' Laurel took Amy's hand gently and drew it towards her, 'Looks a very pretty colour.'

For a moment, Amy was speechless. Laurel's hand was so soft around her own, and now Laurel was looking straight at her. Come on, say something. 'I, um, thanks. I wanted soft colours to cover up the beige.'

'You'll have to show me some time.' Laurel was still smiling at Amy, who cleared her throat awkwardly. Laurel was still holding her hand, and Amy could feel heat creeping through her whole body.

She smiled nervously back, 'Yes, when it's properly finished.'

'I'll look forward to it.' Laurel released her hand.

As Amy was leaving, she said, 'Thank you for coffee, it was very kind of you to invite me.'

'I'm glad you could come.' Something about the way that Laurel spoke those words sent a tingle down Amy's spine.

Standing in the hallway, Amy pulled her coat over her shoulders. Feeling Laurel standing so close unnerved her, and she fumbled with the buttons. 'Here, let me.' Laurel moved close, so close now that Amy could feel the warmth of her breath as she spoke.

As Laurel fastened the top button, her eyes met Amy's straight on, and she smiled at Amy, who could feel the flush spread across her cheeks. Neither of them moved for what seemed an eternity, then Amy could feel herself drawing towards Laurel, her heart beating faster, drumming in her ears.

'There, you're all set.' The moment was gone. Laurel's hand briefly rested on Amy's upper chest, as she smoothed her jacket down. Then suddenly, Laurel was standing back to let Amy get to the door.

As Amy walked along the road, she let out a long breath. For a moment, she had really thought she was going to kiss Laurel. Christ, what was the matter with her? What on earth would Laurel have thought? They were just beginning a friendship, she didn't want to end it before it had really started. But there was something about Laurel. When she was with Laurel, it was as if she was a different person, and she felt that she could truly be herself and relax. Come on, get it together. You've been on your own too long, that's for sure. You need to get out more.

Laurel had been so desperately tempted. It would have been so easy to have moved in, and kissed Amy. She had seen the look Amy had given her. A look of uncertainty, sure, but also one of longing. But Laurel didn't want to rush into anything. They hadn't known each other for very long, and if it was meant to be, well, then... It was going to be interesting to see how things were going to develop...

THREE

Laurel didn't hear from Amy for a while after that morning when she had visited her. After leaving a voicemail and a text message, Laurel decided to leave it for now. She figured that it probably had something to do with that almost kiss. Amy had no doubt freaked out, and had decided to keep her distance. It was such a shame, but there really wasn't anything that Laurel could do about it.

Amy wasn't sure what to do. She valued Laurel's friendship, but the way she was feeling towards Laurel bothered her. She didn't want to do anything that would spoil their friendship, but she also couldn't deny how she felt around Laurel. Anyway, Laurel probably wasn't interested, she certainly hadn't given Amy any reason to think so. She had just been spending too much time with Laurel, so two or three weeks' space would be good for her.

Eventually she decided to call Laurel. 'Amy, how are you? It's been a while.'

Amy sounded awkward, 'Sorry I didn't get back to you sooner, things have been a bit busy.'

'Hey, don't worry about it. It's good to hear from you.'

They had an amicable chat, talking about nothing in particular. Laurel decided to leave it to Amy to suggest getting together again, which she didn't at this point. Having said their goodbyes, that was that for a few weeks.

Amy missed Laurel. She told herself it was good to not see her for a while. She was getting too dependent on seeing her, and she told herself she wasn't going to do that. Not to mention the fact that she almost kissed her. She replayed that moment a thousand times in her head.

It had been Laurel who suggested having lunch. Amy could always say no if she didn't want to. But she had said yes. Laurel said that she'd found a gorgeous tea room in the countryside, and wanted to take Amy there. 'I'll pick you up at two. We can have afternoon tea!'

'Sounds lovely, thank you.'

After she had put the phone down, Amy decided that she ought to have a shower and change her clothes. She had been pottering about, cleaning and tidying, so was wearing sweatpants and an old t-shirt. Having felt a bit lonely that day, she was now excited and looking forward to going out. She chose a pair of smart dark jeans, with a pale blouse and a lightweight jumper in case it was cooler where they were going. As she looked at herself in the mirror, she was pleased with the quick transformation.

Laurel was right on time, and as she opened the door, Amy's nervousness gave way to pleasure at seeing Laurel again. They hugged briefly, before getting into the car. The drive was very relaxing, and neither of them spoke much as they enjoyed the countryside scenery and winding lanes.

The tearoom was set in beautiful gardens, with a stream running along the back. Amy looked around in wonder, 'It's beautiful here. I'd never have known, it's so tucked away.'

'Well, I suppose as you're not local, you probably wouldn't. There are so many places I'd like to show you.'

Amy didn't know what to say for a moment, so she smiled. Eventually, she said, 'That would be lovely, thank you.' After a few more seconds, she said, 'Sorry I didn't get back in touch with you for a while.'

'Hey, don't worry about it. I'm sure you've been busy.' Laurel smiled kindly at her, increasing her sense of guilt.

'Yes, I guess so. You've been very understanding. Thank you.' I wonder if she knows.

'Look, I know it can be hard trying to settle into a new place, where you don't know anyone, and you're trying to find your bearings. But it's okay, and you'll be fine.'

The cream tea was brought over by a grey-haired woman, wearing a white apron and a friendly smile. Her cheeks were red and rosy, she looked like the archetypal farmers wife from one of Amy's childhood books. The scones were enormous, with a generous portion of cream and jam on the side. They tasted as good as they looked, and both women made noises of delight as they ate them, smiling at each other like naughty children as they licked the jam and cream off their fingers. At one point, Amy noticed Laurel watching her, and she wasn't sure what to do. She excused herself, saying she needed to wash her hands.

Once Amy had left the table, Laurel breathed out heavily. How was she going to deal with this, her body was alive with sensation. She found watching Amy licking her fingers had been incredibly erotic, and she just hoped that Amy was oblivious to her reactions. Or would it be a good thing? Amy had almost kissed her that time, maybe she had no idea at all that Laurel fancied her like mad.

While driving home, Laurel was noticeably quiet. Amy thought she seemed quite distracted. Suddenly out of nowhere, a deer ran out in front of them, causing Laurel to break suddenly. Instinctively, Amy reached out and grabbed Laurel's knee, squeezing it tightly. Her hand was frozen for a moment, as though an invisible force was keeping it there. She kept her eyes fixed on the road ahead, but was aware of how still Laurel was. She could feel the taught muscles in Laurel's legs through the material of her trousers. Amy didn't dare look at her, and also knew she would have to move her hand. She told herself it was because of the shock.

Laurel was frozen. Fortunately there hadn't been anyone behind them. Her heart was still pumping furiously, and the deer had long since disappeared, oblivious to the shock it had caused. As her heart rate began to recover, it now had a new sensation. The feel of Amy's hand on Laurel's knee sent warm sensations through her body. As much as she didn't want the moment to end, she knew she couldn't sit in the middle of the road. Laurel turned to Amy, who was still looking straight ahead. As she began to move the car forward, Amy slid her hand back onto her lap, still not saying anything. Eventually, Laurel broke the silence, 'Phew, close call!'

Amy's laugh was a nervous release of energy, 'Certainly was.'

When they arrived back in Worthing, Laurel pulled the car up outside Amy's flat. 'You okay?'

Amy replied softly, 'Yes, fine. Thank you. How about you?'

'I'm fine. You've been very quiet. I know that deer gave us both a shock.'

'It did.' Amy half smiled at Laurel, then turned her head away.

Laurel gently touched Amy's chin, turning her face towards her, searching to try and read what was going on. 'You sure you're okay?'

Amy met her gaze for a while, and nodded, before looking down. Laurel's touch felt electric on her skin, and she hadn't known what to do. It was so gentle, so intimate.

Laurel moved her hand away. Amy didn't seem in a rush to go, but Laurel didn't think she was going to invite her in, either. 'Okay, I'd better be off then.'

Amy seemed to come to, 'Oh, okay. Thank you for today, I had a lovely time.'

Did Amy want her to stay? Goodness knows, she certainly wasn't offering, although she also seemed disappointed that Laurel was going. Maybe Laurel was reading too much into it, she thought.

Amy was hesitant, 'I'd invite you in, but I've got some things to do. Next time, maybe?'

Laurel smiled, 'Yes, of course. I'd like that.'

'Well, thank you again.' Amy leaned over to kiss Laurel goodbye on the cheek. Then she was out of the car, closing the door. She waved at Laurel through the window, then she was gone.

Laurel sat in the car for a few minutes. Was she picking up on something, or just imagining it? Amy's reaction could be explained by the shock of them almost hitting the deer. She didn't really know Amy that well, anyway. Oh well, what will be will be, she thought to herself, as she put the car into gear, and drove off.

Amy closed the front door behind her, and sighed heavily. She kicked her shoes off, and they slid across the wooden floor. What was going on with her. She was in a strange mood, and she didn't like the unfamiliarity of it. Walking over to the window, she was surprised to see Laurel's car outside still. A little fizz of excitement bubbled in Amy's stomach. She could always go outside and invite Laurel in after all. While she was thinking about it, she saw Laurel drive away, and felt a pang of disappointment.

Amy walked into the kitchen to make herself a cup of tea. Her flat, although not that big, was spacious, and the wooden flooring from the hall changed to big pale grey tiles in the kitchen. The white cupboards and pale walls added to the feeling of space in the flat. There was a counter in the middle of the kitchen, with a couple of stools on one side. Usually Amy would eat her meals here, looking out through the big window to the sea. She loved her flat, and believed it was a combination of luck and good timing that she had been able to buy it.

So, what about the timing that had led to her meeting Laurel, she wondered. She couldn't deny that there was something between them, unspoken. But was it just from her side? Yes, Laurel had been friendly towards her. She had smiled at her that first time. It was Laurel who asked to join her, too, and offered to buy her a drink. But all that could be explained by the fact that she was a kind, friendly person. She probably saw that Amy looked like she needed a bit of company. And later on, when she had almost kissed Laurel, Laurel had made no move towards her. Also, it was she who had grabbed Laurel's knee, not the other way around. So perhaps she was reading too much into it. Did it not just confirm that she was lonely, and enjoyed spending time with Laurel? It really didn't have to mean any more than that. Amy told herself that she was tired, and being silly. She would put this from her mind, and enjoy the friendship that she and Laurel had.

FOUR

Amy had invited Laurel out to dinner. 'There's a Thai restaurant I wanted to try out, if you fancy it?'

Laurel's voice was warm and silky down the phone, 'Yes, I'd like that very much, thank you.'

Smiling, Amy said, 'Great, I'll meet you there at eight.'

'Looking forward to it. Until then.'

That evening, they approached the restaurant at the same time, from opposite directions. Smiling at one another as they drew nearer, they hugged as they met. 'You look lovely, Amy.'

'Thank you, so do you.'

They were welcomed in by the couple who ran the restaurant, and shown to their seats.

Sitting down, Laurel said, 'I'm so pleased you invited me. I've missed you.' The words were out before she had realised.

Amy's stomach lurched, surely there was something there, she couldn't just be imagining it. What the hell, 'I've missed you too.'

They looked at each other across the table, and smiled at one other. Then Amy didn't know where to look any more, so turned to her menu.

The air was electric between them, and as Laurel watched Amy studying her menu, she asked, 'So, how have you been?'

Amy looked up, 'Okay, thanks. Busy with work, really. Nothing very interesting. How about you?'

'Not much, mostly I've been catching up on my reading.' And thinking about you.

'I wish I had more time to read. I'm not sure where the time's been going at the moment.' As she spoke, she was trying to gauge the look on Laurel's face.

Had inviting Laurel to dinner been a rash move? Amy told herself not to be so silly, they were friends, and friends went out to dinner. Of course they did.

As Amy relaxed, she really enjoyed her evening with Laurel. The conversation flowed freely, and so did the wine. After her third glass, Amy tried to put her hand over the top to prevent Laurel topping it up. Laurel tried to move her hand away, laughing, and for a moment their fingers touched. Laurel pulled her hand away, saying, 'Sorry. I was getting a bit carried away.'

'Don't be silly. It's just if I have any more wine, you'll have to carry me home!'

'I don't mind.' Laurel gave Amy the longest look, before bursting out laughing, and Amy joining in.

They had ordered sorbet and fruit for dessert. There were just a few pieces of watermelon remaining. As Laurel watched Amy put the sumptuous fruit to her mouth, her lips as pink as the watermelon, she desperately wanted to kiss her, and taste the sweet fruit on her lips for herself. Amy looked up, catching a strange look on Laurel's face, which made her blush and turn away.

Walking home, in a not entirely straight line, Laurel and Amy kept bumping shoulders, and giggling. Amy said, 'I've had such a good time tonight. I can't remember the last time I laughed so much.'

'Me too, I really missed you. We must do this more often.'

'Cheers to that! Oh, I don't have a glass in my hand!' Amy giggled again.

Laurel laughed, 'That's got to be a first tonight!'

'Cheeky! I think you've had as much as me.'

Smiling, Laurel said, 'I think I can handle it a bit better!' She made to run off, as Amy playfully swiped her arm.

When they reached the seafront, they stood and watched the water for a while in the dark. As the moon appeared from behind a cloud, it shined glistening ripples on the surface. They were both quiet as they watched. Eventually, Amy said, 'I'd better head home.'

'Are you sure you're okay to walk on your own? Maybe we should call you a cab.'

Smiling, Amy said, 'No, I'll be fine.'

'Okay, text me when you're home. Thank you for this evening, it's been lovely.'

'Yes, it has. Goodnight Laurel.' Amy liked the sound of Laurel's name on her tongue.

'Goodnight Amelia.' Her own name, seldom spoken in full, sounded exotic in her ear, and sent a tingle down her neck.

They hugged goodbye, and as Laurel kissed Amy's cheek, she felt her linger. As Amy turned her head to kiss Laurel's cheek, Laurel moved, and Amy was kissing her lips. Laurel didn't move, stunned into stillness, then surprise, as Amy didn't pull away. Instead, Amy kissed gently, opening her mouth to Laurel. The kiss was sublime and gentle, like a soak in a deliciously hot bath. Amy didn't know how long it lasted, but as they pulled away from each other, she felt even more drunk than before. 'That was...' Amy couldn't find the words.

'Unexpected?' Laurel offered.

Amy spoke softly, 'Yes. I'm sorry, I shouldn't have-'

'Don't be silly, I'm not sorry at all.' Laurel smiled, and Amy blushed, as her insides fizzed with excitement.

'Okay, I'm gonna go. Night.' She gave a little wave and turned, before she could do or say anything else that would embarrass her.

'Night.' Laurel stood for a while, watching Amy's receding figure as she walked away.

As Laurel walked home, she wished that Amy had been sober. She wondered how the evening might have ended, if that had been the case. Then again, Amy probably would have never kissed her at all. Still, she had been right. There was definitely something between them.

Reaching her front door, Laurel felt her phone vibrate in her pocket. It was Amy. The text read, 'Home now. Had a lovely evening, thank you. Sorry x'

Laurel replied quickly, 'Had a great time too. I'm not sorry at all x'

In the morning, Amy stretched as she opened her eyes. She ran her fingers through her hair, and gently massaged her head. She was feeling a bit muzzy headed, so pushed herself out of bed to go and find herself a glass of water. As she ran the tap, the cascading water sounded loud in the quiet of her flat, and it was somehow also soothing. Getting back into bed, Amy laid her head gently back on the pillows. Her mind wandered back to the previous night. It had been such a wonderful evening, but what had she done? Well, she could blame it on the wine, of course. But she knew full well she wasn't that drunk, just a bit tipsy, maybe. She had nearly kissed Laurel that time in the hallway, so perhaps it was just a matter of time. As far as Laurel was concerned, though, she would blame it on the alcohol.

Laurel awoke after a wonderful, and rather horny, dream about Amy. She could still feel the touch of Amy's lips on her own, and she knew for sure that, at least, hadn't been a dream. She was feeling hot and bothered, partly because she knew that nothing was going to happen. At least not yet, anyway. Amy had seemed embarrassed and sorry about the kiss last night. It may not have been ideal circumstances, but at least Laurel had finally had a chance to feel Amy's lips upon her own. The trouble was, she'd really like there to be more.

Amy decided she needed to focus on work. Maybe find some hobbies. She didn't really have any friends in the area. Except for Laurel. She was still feeling embarrassed about what had happened. She dearly hoped it wouldn't change their friendship. Well, why should it, was it not just a drunken mistake? Laurel seemed fine about it, but Amy couldn't bring herself to make a date to meet up with her again just yet.

FIVE

Anna had recently joined Amy's office, and their desks were opposite one another. They got along well together, and Amy found that work was more enjoyable now there was a slightly more sociable aspect to the job. Over lunch one day, Anna suggested, 'Why don't you come out to dinner with me and Sam one evening. Sam's mate Dave could do with getting out more, I think you'd get on well. What d'ya think?'

'What, like a double date?'

Anna laughed, 'Sort of, but just informal. I'm not setting you up on a blind date.'

Amy thought about it for a moment. Then, 'Okay, why not!'

'Great, I'll sort something out.'

Anna had told Amy that they would all meet for a drink first at The Goose, on the seafront. Amy had walked past the bar many times, but not been inside. The steps at the front led up to long wooden tables and benches outside, perfect for a drink on a summers evening, complete with a sea view. As Amy approached, she could see Anna, but as she scanned the bench, she couldn't see any guys, so assumed that Sam and Dave hadn't arrived yet. Anna stood to greet her, 'Hi, glad you could make it.'

'Hi, are the others not here yet?'

'Dave's running a bit late.' Turning to her right, Anna said, 'Amy, this is Sam. Sam, Amy.'

'Oh, hi. Pleased to meet you.' Amy hoped her pink cheeks weren't too obvious. She'd just assumed Sam was a guy, she'd not remembered Anna saying otherwise. She shook Sam's hand, and she smiled warmly at her.

To cover her embarrassment, Amy asked, 'Would either of you like a drink?'

'No thanks, we're sorted.'

'I'll just get one, then. Back In a minute.'

As Amy walked inside towards the bar, she was glad to have a moment to calm herself down. Why had she just assumed Sam was a guy? Never mind, live and learn, and all that. Having got herself a drink, Amy headed back to their bench outside. Sam and Anna were talking to a guy who hadn't been there when she had left. Now, was it safe to assume that might be Dave?

'Here she is.' Anna introduced them, 'Dave, this is Amy.'

Dave stood up, offering his hand, 'Pleased to meet you.'

'Likewise. Anna's told me lots about you.' They shook hands, and Dave's felt slightly clammy in Amy's warm hand.

'Not too much, I hope!'

Phew, well Dave seemed as nervous as Amy felt, she decided. He was a nice looking guy, medium build, with short dark hair. Amy thought he was probably a good few years younger than her. Well, that didn't matter, they were making up a social group, not on a date. With that thought, Amy began to relax. With introductions finished, and drinks all round, the four of them sat down chatting comfortably.

'Well, I didn't expect to see you here!'

Amy was surprised by the voice that she hadn't heard for a while, and immediately her cheeks flushed.

'Oh, hi.'

Laurel spoke again, 'It's so good to see you. You look well, how are you?'

Amy couldn't really get up to greet her, as she was penned in at the end of the bench. 'Good thanks. Busy. How are you?' She really must think of something else to say to Laurel, other than being busy. She had told Laurel countless times how bored she could get, it would be obvious to her that she was lying. Unless she counted the fact that she was busy thinking about Laurel constantly.

'Very well thank you. Just off to the cinema, I'm meeting a friend.' Laurel could see how uncomfortable Amy looked. After a long pause, 'Well, I won't keep you, I can see you're busy. Call me, let's meet up.'

'Yes, I'd like that. Enjoy your film.' Was that a pang of jealousy at the thought of Laurel going to the cinema with someone else?

'Bye.' Laurel gave a lingering look at Amy, before turning and walking away.

Anna and Sam watched the exchange with fascination. There was another unspoken conversation happening between Laurel and Amy, and they were interested to know more. After Laurel had disappeared, Anna said, 'She seems nice.'

Amy cleared her throat, 'Yes, she is. Sorry, I didn't introduce you. That was Laurel.'

'And Laurel is?'

'Just a friend.' End of conversation.

Anna and Sam, sitting opposite Amy, could see her flushed cheeks, her dilated pupils. Yes, there was definitely a story there. Maybe Anna would find out a bit more over lunch one day.

Laurel had been surprised to see Amy, and her reaction took her somewhat by surprise. She had a longing pang of want and need, which she felt at her core. Fuck. That hadn't happened in a long time. It was no use thinking of what might have been, and Laurel wasn't one for dreaming idle fantasies. She was usually pretty matter of fact about things. Amy hadn't been in contact since that kiss, and the more time that passed, the less Laurel was expecting to hear from her. In that moment when they had locked eyes again, Laurel knew she had fallen for Amy. Damn.

Amy sipped her drink quietly. It had been good to see Laurel, hear her voice. She had missed her. And now she felt bad that she hadn't been in contact since that night. And oh, that kiss.

Outside the cinema, Laurel could see her friend waiting expectantly. As she caught sight of her, they smiled at one another. 'Laurel, so good to see you, how are you?' Serena enveloped her in a hug.

'Good to see you too. I'm fine.'

Serena held Laurel's shoulders at arms length, her eyes searching Laurel's face, 'Are you sure?'

Laurel pasted on a smile, 'Yes, of course. Just saw someone I wasn't expecting to, that's all.'

'Well, we've all been there!' Serena linked her arm through Laurel's. 'Come on, I've got the tickets, let's get a drink in the bar, and you can tell me all about her.'

Serena and Laurel sat on a sofa, tucked away in the corner of the bar. 'So?'

They had been friends for many years, and Laurel knew she wasn't going to get away with brushing it off as nothing. 'It's silly, really.'

'I'm sure it's not. So how did you meet her?' Serena tended to be very direct.

Laurel relayed the story of how she had met Amy. When she got to the end of it, Serena noticed how her eyes glazed over.

'Oh boy, you've got it bad. I've never seen you like this before, I want to meet this woman!'

Laurel smiled sadly at her friend, 'I'm not sure whether we're even friends now, really. She looked so shocked to see me earlier.'

'It can be a tricky step, moving from a friendship to a relationship.'

'I felt a connection from the moment I saw her. But I'm not stupid, I didn't expect her to take one look and fall for me. I was prepared that we may have a friendship, and nothing more.' She paused for a while. 'I didn't expect to fall in love with her.'

Serena took her hand, and squeezed it. 'Give it some time. Now you've seen each other again, she may decide to contact you.'

Laurel sighed, 'I don't think so. Anyway, enough about me, how are things with you?'

At work the following week, Anna was chatting with Amy over lunch. 'So, what did you think of Dave?'

Amy smiled, 'He's a sweet guy. I really liked him.'

'That's good. I really enjoyed the evening. It's fun to go out together in a group for a change.'

'Sam's lovely. How long have you two been together?'

Anna was smiling as she answered, 'Over three years now.'

'You're very sweet together.'

Anna laughed, 'Thanks. So, erm, that woman you spoke to. Laura, was it?'

Amy's face straightened. 'Laurel.'

'Sorry, it's none of my business. I just wondered....' She felt bad now for bringing it up, it was obviously a sore point.

'Like I said, she's just a friend.'

'If you say so.' Damn, I need to keep my opinions to myself. At the look on Amy's face, she knew she had gone too far. 'I'm so sorry, it's none of my business. Please forgive me.'

Amy paused for a moment. 'It's okay. Well, we'd better get back to work.' She hurriedly packed her things up, and disappeared out of the staff room.

Sam was always telling Anna she should keep her nose out of other people's business. It was just that she thought Amy might like someone to talk to. Someone who would understand.

As the weeks went by, Laurel stopped expecting to hear from Amy. There were many occasions when she had picked up her phone to text Amy, started to type a message, only to delete it again. What would be the point. She would have to accept that their friendship was probably over now. She was due to be travelling again soon, that would help to take her mind off things.

SIX

Amy was enjoying a pleasant evening with Dave. They weren't dating, but they were becoming good friends. Amy was very relaxed in his company. She could see the way Dave was looking at her, and she really did like him, but neither had given any suggestion that they wanted something more. It was good that she was increasing her circle of friends now. She and Anna socialised more, as well as getting together with Sam and Dave. So why did Laurel keep popping into her mind.

Over coffee, Amy said, 'I'm so sorry, I've just remembered something. I have to go.'

Dave was put out. 'Really? Isn't it a bit late?' He was enjoying his evening with Amy, and he had hoped that things were going to go a bit further tonight.

'As you say, it is getting late. I'll be in touch, thank you for this evening.' They had already paid the bill, and were taking their time over coffee. Standing, she leaned down to give Dave a chaste kiss on the cheek, leaving him dumbstruck at the table. All he could do was watch after her as she collected her coat, and left.

Amy knocked gently on the door, her heart hammering in her chest. It was getting late, maybe she shouldn't have come, what was she doing? She must have had too much to drink tonight. It would be better to leave, and sleep on things, see how she felt in the morning. She didn't want to do something she would later regret. As she turned to walk away, Amy heard the door open behind her.

Laurel looked surprised, and also concerned. 'Amy, are you okay?'

'Erm, yes. I'm fine. I don't really know how to explain why I'm here.'

'Well, come in. Let's talk inside.'

Amy was flustered, 'Thank you, I'm sorry for turning up so late. I was about to leave when you opened the door. I hope I didn't get you out of bed.' She ran her eyes down Laurel's body, taking in the white cotton pyjamas. The lamp on the hall table behind Laurel silhouetted her figure through her nightwear.

'It's fine. I was just reading.' Amy noticed a pair of glasses on Laurel's head, which drew her hair away from her face.

'I didn't know you wore glasses.'

'Only for reading.' She smiled at Amy, her beautiful lips curling up at the edges. Oh boy. 'Would you like a drink?'

Amy's mouth was suddenly feeling very dry. 'Yes please. If it's not too much trouble.'

Laurel headed towards the kitchen, and Amy followed her, watching the curve of her hips as she moved. What the fuck am I doing?

'I make a mean hot chocolate if you fancy it?'

'That sounds lovely, thank you.' Laurel removed the glasses from the top of her head, and her hair fell loose. Placing her glasses on the counter, Amy watched as Laurel made them both drinks, and poured the steaming hot chocolate into a pair of mugs.

Handing a mug to Amy, Laurel said, 'Let's go and sit on the sofa, it'll be warmer in the lounge.'

Once they were settled down, they each took a sip of their drink. 'This is delicious. Thank you. I'm sorry for just turning up like this, and so late.'

'I'm not.' Laurel looked at Amy, her eyes locking onto her own. Amy swallowed hard, and her heart started thumping in her chest again. She quietly sipped at her drink, glad of something to keep her hands and mouth occupied. For a while, they both sat in silence.

Laurel had been surprised to see Amy on her doorstep so late, but she knew why she had come. She may have doubted herself, but now she was glad the wait was soon going to be over. A tingle of excitement ran up her spine and along her scalp.

50

Finishing her drink, Laurel sat back on the sofa. Amy followed her lead, hoping that she looked more relaxed than she felt. They were sitting very close, their hands almost touching on the sofa. Her face feeling flushed, Amy said, 'I don't know how to explain why I'm here. I was out having dinner with Dave tonight. You know, the guy at The Goose.'

'Oh.' Laurel's stomach felt instantly heavy.

'Then I suddenly told him that I'd remembered something, and I had to go.' Amy pulled a funny face.

Laurel laughed, her stomach feeling lighter. 'Did you tell him what you had remembered?'

For a moment, Amy looked serious. 'I wouldn't know how to put it into words.'

Laurel put her head on one side, 'Then how would you put it?' She could feel the electricity buzzing between them.

Amy looked at Laurel, surprised, and before she had time to think about what she was doing, her body took over, and she learned forward, and kissed Laurel. Laurel kissed back passionately, and put her arms around Amy, pulling her close.

Laurel was ecstatic. Finally. She knew it was going to happen, that first time that Amy had looked at her. She couldn't explain it in any way, other than it was a knowing, somewhere deep inside her.

After an age, they pulled apart, both breathing heavily. Laurel's voice was breathy, 'I've waited so long for you to do that.'

Amy was surprised, 'Really?'

'Oh, yes. I can't tell you how many times I've wanted to kiss you. You know that night after dinner was more than a drunken kiss, don't you?'

Amy spoke quietly, 'I really didn't know.'

Laurel looked at her intently, 'It was beautiful, but I wanted you to kiss me when you were sober.'

'Oh.' Amy was trying to get her head around this new information. 'You know, I can't quite believe I came here. It's just that I haven't been able to stop thinking about you.'

With that, Laurel kissed Amy, their arms around one another, holding each other close. When they drew apart again, Laurel was the first to speak, 'Your lips taste so sweet.'

Amy smiled shyly. 'So, um, when did you first want to kiss me?'

'Since the day I met you.'

Surprise was written all over Amy's face. 'Why didn't you say something before?'

Laurel took Amy's hand in hers, 'The time had to be right. If I'd said something to you that first day, how do you think you would have reacted?'

Amy smiled, 'I guess I would have been quite surprised.'

Laurel laughed. 'I probably wouldn't have seen you for dust. I knew that I couldn't rush things with you.'

'Even so, if I hadn't made the first move, it may have never happened.'

Laurel gave Amy a look that made her stomach turn over with excitement. 'I can assure you, it was definitely going to happen! Also, I can say that you were worth waiting for.'

'That's so sweet.' Amy kissed Laurel on the lips.

After chatting for a while, Amy said, 'I think I'd better go now. I don't know what time it is, but can we meet up tomorrow?'

'Of course. But look, why don't you stay here tonight?'

Amy looked worried. 'I think I should head off.'

Laurel put her hand on Amy's arm, 'We don't have to do anything. You can sleep in the spare room if you'd be more comfortable with that. Personally, I'd rather you share my bed, though. Come on, I'll lend you a pair of pjs!'

Amy couldn't help but laugh at the hopeful look on Laurel's face. 'Okay, I'll stay. Thank you.'

Having put on a pair of pale blue linen pyjamas, Amy slipped under the duvet cover. She was feeling nervous and excited at the same time. Laurel walked into the bedroom, and slipped under the covers, next to Amy. They kissed, and Laurel could feel Amy trembling slightly. She sat back, stroking Amy's hair. 'You okay?'

Amy nodded. 'Just a bit nervous.'

'We won't do anything until you're ready.'

Amy looked in Laurel's eyes, 'Thank you. It's not that I don't want to, it's just that it's harder than I thought it would be.'

'Hey, don't look so worried, it's fine.' Laurel kissed Amy briefly on the cheek, and lent over to turn off the bedside lamp. 'Goodnight.'

'Night.' Amy turned onto her side, and Laurel snuggled up behind her, putting her arms around Amy.

Amy's head was buzzing with the events of the evening, and she also couldn't help smiling to herself. Tucked up in Laurel's arms, she felt so safe and at home. Laurel's breath slowed down, and soon she was asleep. Eventually, sleep got the better of Amy too, and she drifted off.

As Amy woke up, rubbing her bleary eyes, she turned her head to look at Laurel. She watched the gentle rise and fall of Laurel's chest as she slept, her dark brown, shoulder length hair half covering her face. She gently stroked Laurel's hair back over her ear, so she could look at her. Amy ran her hand through her own cropped honey blond hair, tussled and wayward as usual.

Laurel opened her eyes, and immediately a sleepy smile crossed her face, 'Morning, gorgeous!'

Amy beamed back at her, 'Good morning to you, too!' Amy kissed Laurel, and soon the kiss heated up, and their hands were all over one another.

Amy started to pull back, and Laurel asked, 'Are you okay?'

'Yes, I'm fine. I'm just trying to adjust to the sudden change in our friendship. I don't want to rush anything.'

Laurel smiled, 'Hey, whatever you need. I'm very good at being patient!'

'Thank you for being so understanding.'

'Come on, let's go and get some breakfast. Maybe after that we can go for a walk if you fancy it?'

Amy smiled at Laurel, 'That sounds perfect.'

Over a breakfast of toast, orange juice and coffee, Laurel was looking at Amy across the table. 'What?'

Laurel smiled, 'You are so fucking sexy. With your hair all tousled, looking like butter wouldn't melt!'

Amy couldn't help laughing. 'I've never been able to get my hair to do quite what I want it to.'

'Not acknowledging the compliment, then!'

Amy looked shy for a moment, 'Thank you. You look beautiful this morning.'

'Why, thank you.' Laurel beamed at Amy, then took her hand, kissing the back of it.

Walking along the seafront, Laurel held Amy's hand. 'Is this okay?'

Amy smiled back, 'Yes, it feels nice.'

For a while, they walked along quietly, listening to the waves washing up onto the pebbles, and the squawk of the seagulls above.

'So.'

'Yes?' Amy turned to look at Laurel.

'What now?'

Amy slowed her pace, then stopped. 'I don't know. I really haven't thought any of this through.'

Laurel took Amy's hands in hers, 'Would it help if I told you how I feel?'

Amy was a bit hesitant, 'Okay.'

'I've fancied you since I first saw you walk past the cafe and you looked at me. I even tried to keep my distance, but I couldn't stay away. If you need to go slowly, I can do that, whatever you want.'

Amy looked lovingly at Laurel, and Laurel's heart flipped. 'You are so sweet and understanding.'

'But I should also tell you that I desperately want to fuck you!'

Amy couldn't help but laugh out loud. 'Laurel! Bloody hell!'

Laurel threw her hands up, 'Hey, I just want to be honest!'

Amy laughed, 'What am I getting myself into?'

'Let me show you...' Laurel pulled Amy into an embrace, kissing her tenderly, and holding her close.

When they eventually pulled apart, Amy said, 'Wow.'

'You said it.'

Before either of them could say anything else, a voice said, 'Hello, how are you?'

Amy jumped, and let go of Laurel's hand, 'Hey, hello.'

'Sorry, I didn't mean to surprise you.'

'No, you didn't. Um, Rebecca, this is Laurel. Laurel, Rebecca.'

They smiled at one another, 'Nice to meet you.'

After a bit of small talk, they said their goodbyes, and Amy and Laurel started to head back home. Laurel had noticed that Amy seemed quiet since they had seen Rebecca. 'You okay?'

'Yes, of course.' Amy hadn't tried to hold Laurel's hand again, and Laurel decided to wait. Well, she thought it would be better to. Seeing the way that Amy had reacted when they bumped into Rebecca, Laurel was concerned that their relationship was about to take a step backwards.

Amy was feeling a bit awkward since she had seen Rebecca. Had Rebecca seen them holding hands? Oh god, she might have seen them kissing. Would she tell people, and what would they think. Not that it was anyone's business, anyway.

When they were back in Laurel's kitchen, she asked Amy if she would like a drink. 'Coffee, please.'

'I think I'll join you.'

Amy was watching Laurel as she busied herself making the drinks. She was so self assured, a quality that she had often noticed and admired in Laurel. Laurel turned to see Amy looking at her, and as she smiled, Amy blushed.

Sitting at the counter with their coffees, the steam rising upwards, Laurel said, 'I couldn't help noticing how quiet you were after we saw your friend.'

Amy shuffled uncomfortably on her chair. 'She's just a colleague. I guess it felt weird. I don't know what I thought would happen.' She paused, running her hand through her tousled hair, 'Oh god, I really like you, and I don't want to mess you around.'

Seeing Amy looking flustered, and her hair cutely dishevelled, Laurel just melted. Moving towards Amy, Laurel's voice was soft and low, 'At this moment, you can mess me around as much as you like.' She kissed Amy very lightly on the lips.

'Oh, shit. Come here.' Amy pulled Laurel towards her, kissing her passionately, and running her hands through her hair and down her back. She began unbuttoning Laurel's blouse, and then pulled her own top off, over her head. Laurel began kissing down the front of Amy's chest, whilst massaging her breasts, causing Amy to throw her head back and moan noises of appreciation. Laurel was so turned on by the turn of events, and she undid Amy's bra, freeing her breasts. 'Fuck, you have gorgeous tits!'

Amy laughed, and the sound was music to Laurel's ears. Then she felt the delicious sensation of Amy kissing her neck, then her breasts. Oh, how she had longed for this. As things heated up between them, Laurel breathed, 'Shall we go upstairs?'

Amy looked at Laurel shyly and nodded, and Laurel took her hand, leading the way. They were about half way up the stairs when there was a knock on the door. Amy stopped where she was. Laurel said, 'Ignore it. Whoever it is will go away.' She continued up the stairs, but the knocking was insistent.

Then from the other side of the door, 'I know you're there, Laurel, I can hear you.'

'Damn it.'

Amy said, 'I think you'd better answer it. I'll wait in the bedroom.'

Reluctantly, Laurel nodded, and put her blouse back on, fastening it hurriedly as she went back downstairs. She wanted to get rid of whoever it was as soon as possible.

As Amy sat nervously on the bed, she couldn't make out any of the conversation going on downstairs. It obviously hadn't been as easy to get rid of the person as Laurel had thought. So do I wait here indefinitely, or what? Amy was getting agitated now. Not knowing who was downstairs, it might be awkward if she suddenly made an appearance now. Amy had since redressed, and decided that if she was quiet, she could sneak out, and leave Laurel a note.

Laurel made her excuses as soon as she could, and dashed upstairs to find Amy. Where the hell had she got to. She wasn't in the bedroom or the bathroom. Then, on the bedside cabinet, she noticed a note. 'Wasn't sure what to do, so thought it best to leave. See you soon, love A x'. Shit. Why had Natalie chosen that precise moment to come round. Just as things were happening, Laurel couldn't believe the appalling timing. She should have just ignored the door, what on earth possessed her to open it?

Laurel wasn't getting any answer from Amy's phone. Shit. Well, she had already left a message, so she would just have to wait for Amy to get back in touch.

Amy had taken the long walk home. She was glad to have a bit of headspace. Since last night, things felt like they were moving quickly. Not that Laurel had rushed her in any way. In fact, she had been very relaxed about the whole thing. Then she remembered Laurel's comment about wanting to fuck her, and she couldn't help laughing to herself. The thought of it excited her, and also made her rather nervous. A part of Amy longed for Laurel, but was this all a mistake?

She loved spending time with Laurel, and valued her friendship. If they took things further, what if it didn't work out? Was it best to keep their friendship. On the other hand, it had already turned into something more. Amy had made the first move herself, although Laurel had made it very clear how she felt about her. Maybe it was inevitable now. Having slept in Laurel's bed, Amy had felt so safe and comfortable. And when she kissed her, well... Oh god, what am I going to do?

SEVEN

At work, Amy had begun talking to Anna more. She had been spending more time with her when she and Dave made up a foursome with Anna and Sam. 'Are you okay?'

Amy looked up at Anna, 'Yes, fine thanks.'

'If you so say so.'

Amy sighed heavily, 'Sorry. There is something.'

'Well, I can see that. So tell me.'

'It's awkward. What with Sam and Dave being friends.'

Anna was understanding, 'Look, I won't say anything to Dave.'

After hesitating, Amy started, 'Do you remember the first time we went out. And a woman spoke to me outside the pub on the seafront.'

'Yes. The, just a friend. I knew it!'

'Let me finish.'

'Sorry.' Anna looked chastened.

'It's just. It just kind of happened.'

'You slept with her?'

'No. Well, um, yes. No, not in that way.'

Anna was confused, 'What are you talking about?'

'We've kissed, and I'm really attracted to her. Something nearly happened, and now I don't know what to do.'

'Okay, so what's the problem?'

Amy was astounded by Anna's lightheartedness. 'Well, she's my friend. If we take things further, then what?'

'Ooh, sounds like it'll be good finding out!'

'You're not helping.' Amy was getting cross now.

'Sorry. It's just that, well, that evening, Sam and I could see there was something between you. You could have cut the air with a knife.'

'Really?' Amy looked hopeful and excited.

'Trust me. Look, things have obviously gone further anyway, so what have you got to lose?'

Amy's face was stern, 'A friendship, if it doesn't work.'

Anna leaned in, 'Or you could gain an amazing relationship. It sounds like things are too far forward to go back. Don't overthink it, just let yourself go.'

'That's what got me into this in the first place! Also, I don't know what to say to Dave. We are only friends, but I think he'd like it to be more. I really like him, but not in that way.'

'You've not given him reason to think that, so don't worry about it. One thing at a time. Go and talk to Laurel.'

Laurel still hadn't heard from Amy by the following day. Maybe she should she go round to Amy's. Although if Amy needed space, that may not be the best idea. But Amy had turned up on her doorstep. Amy had made the first move. Oh, how Laurel wanted her. Lost in thought, Laurel was brought into the present by a ping on her mobile phone. Amy. Her heart started to beat faster. 'Sorry I haven't been in touch sooner. My mind has been all over the place. I don't want to mess you around, but I don't know what to do. A x.'

Laurel sighed. Immediately she replied, 'Let's talk. Shall we meet at our cafe at noon?' She pressed send.

Having received a yes from Amy, Laurel was relieved. It was ten thirty, and for Laurel noon couldn't come soon enough.

When Amy arrived at the cafe, Laurel was already seated. 'Hi.' She stood to hug Amy.

Seated opposite one another, the waitress took their order and disappeared again. Laurel longed to touch Amy, but she could see how nervous Amy looked. Oh shit, she was dreading the conversation she thought might follow.

'How are you?' Amy fidgeted in her chair.

'I'm good. I was so pleased to hear from you.' Laurel looked deep into Amy's eyes.

'Sorry I left the other day. I wasn't sure what to do, and started to freak out.' Amy looked down at the tablecloth, focusing on some stray grains of demerara sugar.

Having brought their drinks, the waitress left again.

'Like I said, we can go at whatever pace you want. I'm not going to push you. But, you did turn up at my door. I know this is something you want.'

Amy looked up at Laurel, and smiled, although it was slightly strained. 'I'm afraid that it will change things with us. I don't want to ruin our friendship.'

Laurel spoke softly, 'I think it's gone beyond that now.'

Amy sighed, 'I think it was a mistake, coming round to yours that night.'

Laurel was stung, and sat back in her chair. She couldn't keep the hurt out of her voice, 'I understand that you're nervous, but I didn't realise you regretted what happened.'

Amy's eyes welled up, 'I didn't mean it like that. Oh, I don't know what I mean.'

Laurel felt a surge of affection for Amy, and smiled as she said, 'You know, I think we should just do it, now. We've gone over the line, so let's just get it out of our systems. We fuck once, and if either of us thinks it was a mistake, we call it a day.'

Amy couldn't help but smile, 'Really! You think that's the answer?'

'I can't stop thinking about you, and now we've started, I think we just have to go for it. No strings, just a bit of fun.' Laurel knew that for her part, it was more than fun. She was falling hard for Amy, but she wanted to keep things as light hearted as possible.

'I've never done anything like this before.'

Laurel held Amy's hand across the table, 'Hey, there's a first time for everything.'

Having finished their coffees, Laurel suggested they go for a walk along the seafront. After walking along side by side for about a mile, Laurel took Amy's hand, and she didn't draw it away.

Amy felt comfortable walking hand in hand with Laurel. When she was with her, she didn't question how she felt. It was only when they were apart, that Amy started to over think their burgeoning relationship. Maybe Laurel was right, they were unattached grown ups, why not have a bit of fun. But again, that little voice at the back of Amy's mind was asking, what if it ends your friendship?

They had walked quite a long way, in the direction of Goring. There was shelter from a group of trees, and Laurel pulled Amy towards her. 'I really want to kiss you.'

Amy looked into Laurel's eyes, 'I really want you to.'

Their lips met, and they melted into one another. As they kissed, Laurel turned her around, so that Amy was now leaning her back against the trunk of a large tree. Amy didn't resist, she went with it, feeling enveloped and loved by Laurel. Their kisses became more passionate, their hands everywhere, and Amy's stomach tightened as she felt Laurel's hand sliding down the front of her trousers, and inside her pants. She pulled Laurel closer, at this point not wanting her to stop. Now the decision was being taken out of her hands, and she really wanted this, and she desperately wanted Laurel. She was so wet and ready, and Laurel gasped appreciatively as she slid her fingers into Amy, watching for her response. 'Aaah.' Amy was turning to putty under Laurel's expert touch.

'Oh my god, you are so hot. You make me so fucking horny.'

Amy couldn't speak, all she was capable of was making heavy breaths and groans. She had even lost the ability to wonder whether anyone would be able to see them. They kissed as though their lives depended on it, and Amy's body responded all over, as she held Laurel tightly. Laurel had been moving inside her so slowly to begin with, and gradually increased the speed, bringing her towards the inevitable climax. As the sensations overtook her body, Amy's knees weakened. Laurel held her, kissing her again, and gently withdrawing her fingers. All Amy could eventually say was, 'Fuck!'

Laurel's face searched Amy's, 'You okay?'

Amy nodded. 'Yes.'

'Do you want to come back to mine?' Laurel's eyes were hooded, and full of passion.

'Yes.'

It seemed to Amy to take forever to get back to Laurel's, but as soon as they were inside the door, they were back in one another's arms. Then Laurel led Amy to her bedroom, and they began undressing one another. Amy's body was still buzzing from what had just happened. It was only then that she thought about what might have happened if someone had seen them. She let out a giggle. 'Are you ticklish?'

Amy shook her head, still laughing, 'I can't believe what we just did. And in public!'

'Sorry, you just do something to me.'

'Well, I'm going to do something to you now.' Amy looked at Laurel playfully, and her insides melted.

'Anything you want, sweetheart.'

Amy removed the last of Laurel's clothes and pushed her back on the bed. She kissed and caressed the whole of Laurel's body, saving the best until last. When she eventually moved down between Laurel's thighs, Laurel was so turned on that her whole body responded to the soft touch of Amy's tongue, and it wasn't long before her body bucked and shuddered as she climaxed.

They made love all afternoon, and eventually fell asleep, the afternoon sun sending a shaft of light across the bedroom.

Amy was aware of movement, and opened her eyes to see Laurel sitting up in bed, looking at her. Laurel beamed at Amy, and leaned down to kiss her. 'Hello. Have I been asleep long?'

'Not that long. I've just woken up. You have a very sexy morning voice.'

Amy looked concerned, 'We didn't sleep until morning, did we?'

Laurel laughed, 'I should say a just woken up voice! How are you feeling?'

For a moment, Amy felt shy and blushed as she remembered what had happened that afternoon. The way that Laurel had caressed her, and kissed her. And the things she had done to Laurel. It was almost like it wasn't her, and she had been watching someone else. But the sensations in her body, and the passion she felt in her heart, she knew were most definitely hers. 'I feel wonderful. How about you?'

Laurel smiled at Amy, stroking her hair back from her face, 'I've never felt happier.'

Amy smiled back, 'Well, I guess that's the friendship fucked, quite literally!'

They both fell into fits of laughter.

THE END

Thank you for reading, I really hope you enjoyed it.

About Sarah

Sarah loves to read and write when she has the time. Often to be found in cafes and on seafront walks.

If you would like to find out more, please visit www.sarahpond.co.uk

Other books by Sarah Pond

CITRUS BLOSSOM

She didn't know when it started, when things had changed. Had there been signs, and she had been too caught up in other things to see them… Maybe it was just a phase, or was she starting to lose it? Or maybe she was beginning to find herself. Perhaps she could just give in to it, let herself go…

When Olivia moves from Cornwall to London to begin a new career, and meets her new boss, Jasmine, she has no idea how it's going to turn her world upside down. She had longed for the excitement of London, but what she hadn't expected was the passion and heartache when everything that she thought she knew about herself is questioned.

In a world of expectation, including your own, following your heart can sometimes be the hardest thing to do.

HIBISCUS

When Rachel has her first holiday in years after starting her art gallery, she was expecting some time to herself to relax. She didn't expect to have a passionate affair, and would never have dreamed it would have been with a woman.

Lea loves living in her quiet costal village. When she meets the woman staying at a nearby cottage, she thinks she's met the love of her life.

Despite their connection, Rachel thinks it's just a holiday fling. Thinking that they'll never see each other again, fate has other ideas. But with such different outlooks and lifestyles, not to mention the distance between them, could a relationship ever work?

THE WOMAN IN THE PYJAMAS

When she woke up that morning, she had no idea that today was going to be the day that would change her life.

It was only looking back, that Daisy realised that the day she had locked herself out of her house, still wearing her pyjamas under her clothes, was the day that things had begun to change.

After a life of routine, sensible clothes and with a marriage behind her, 40 year old Daisy knows it's time to start doing things differently. Her daughter is still her priority, but maybe she can start to let her hair down a bit...

All available as ebook and paperback

www.sarahpond.co.uk

Printed in Great Britain
by Amazon